Kathie Lee Gifford
Party Animals

For Cody and Cassidy—
my favorite Party Animals

9 8 7 6 5 4 3 2 1
Digit on the right indicates the number of this printing.

Library of Congress Control Number: 2009940845
ISBN 978-0-7624-3889-1

Cover and interior design by Frances J. Soo Ping Chow
Edited by Kelli Chipponeri
Typography: Jheri Curls, Love Ya Like A Sister, and Whitney

Published by Running Press Kids, an imprint of
Running Press Book Publishers
2300 Chestnut Street
Philadelphia, PA 19103-4371

Visit us on the web!
www.runningpress.com

Kathie Lee Gifford
PARTY ANIMALS

Illustrated by
Peter Bay Alexandersen

RP|KIDS
PHILADELPHIA · LONDON

Lucy Goosy was thrilled. She was filled with delight.
Her birthday was coming . . . who should she invite?

She wanted her party to be simply the best,
so she had to be careful when choosing each guest.

"I can't invite Pig. She'll eat all the food."

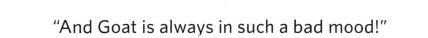
"And Goat is always in such a bad mood!"

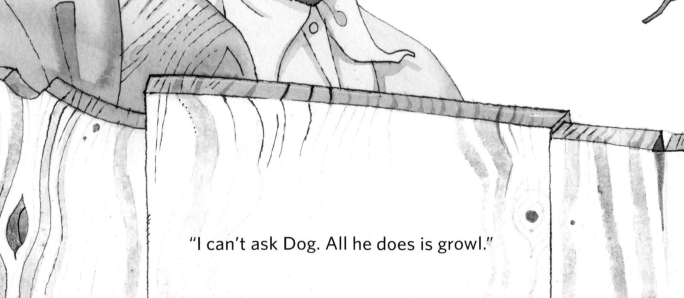

"I can't ask Dog. All he does is growl."

"I know what I'll do. I'll ask the Wise Owl!"
"Whoooo?"

"Owl, if Cat comes, all she'll do is purr.
And she has that bad habit of licking her fur."

"I see," Owl said. "But what about Lamb?"
"What?" cried Goose. "She's more boring than I am!"

"Sheep is too dumb, so I'd like to ask Horse,
but all he does is graze on green grass, of course."

"No one is worse than that messy Raccoon,
except maybe Fox who just howls at the moon!"

"There must be someone you'd like to come," said Owl.
But sadly the Goose could think of no one.

"And that Bee is too busy to leave his beehive."

"That silly Old Hen just keeps pecking around,
and that Gopher keeps digging those holes in the ground!"

"How about Donkey?" asked Owl.
"No, he's such a dud."

"All that Cow does is moo and chew on her cud!"

"I can't stand that Rooster with that ratty hairdo,
who just struts around going
'cock-a-doodle, cock-a-doodle,
cock-a-doodle-doodle-do!'"

By now Lucy Goosy was becoming alarmed.
"Why, I used to think I had good friends on this farm."

"Well, perhaps it's your fault," said the Owl, always wise.
"All you seem to do well is criticize."

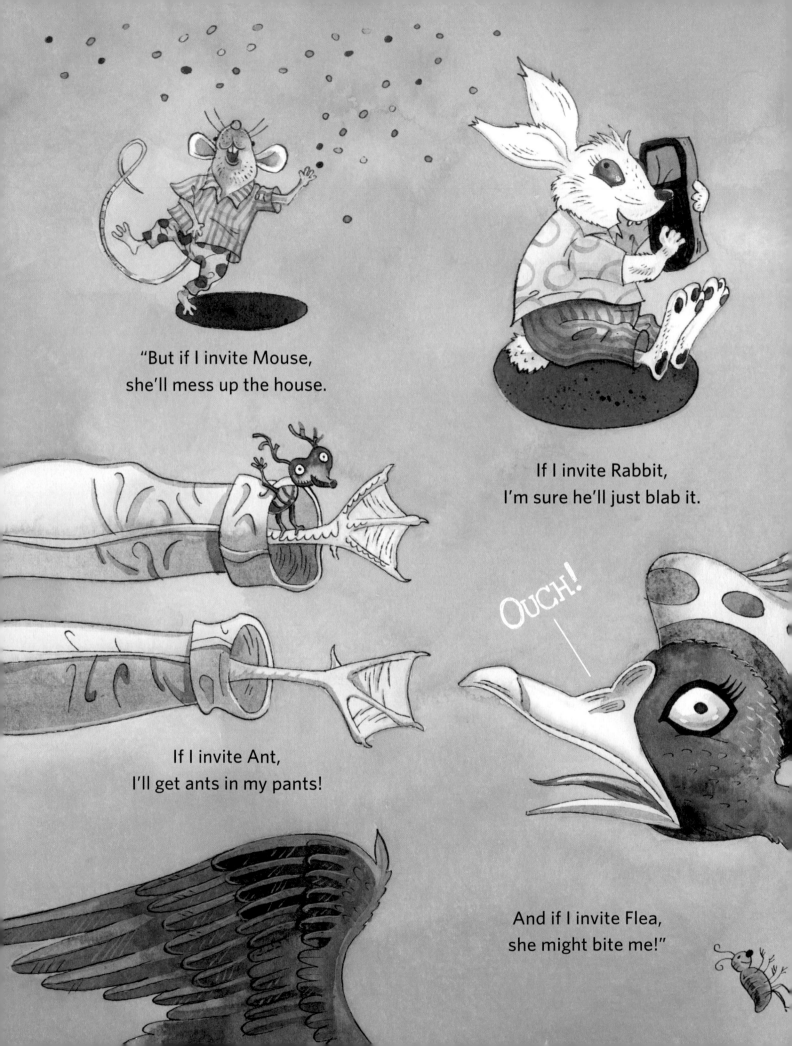

"But if I invite Mouse,
she'll mess up the house.

If I invite Rabbit,
I'm sure he'll just blab it.

If I invite Ant,
I'll get ants in my pants!

OUCH!

And if I invite Flea,
she might bite me!"

The wise old owl simply shook his head.
Then he cleared his throat, and he gently said,

"No one is perfect, you know, even you.
If you want my advice, this is what you should do . . ."

"Invite every animal on the farm to come!
When we all get together, it will be so much fun.
Oh, can't you imagine the look in their eyes,
when suddenly each comes to realize
each one's been invited to share your special day?
No one will forget Lucy Goosy's birthday!"

Lucy Goosy bowed her head in shame.
"You mean each one is special because no one's the same?"

"Yes, each has a gift that no one else gives.
So let's celebrate how different each one of us is!"

lyrics

Lucy Goosy was thrilled. She was filled with delight.
Her birthday was coming . . . who should she invite?
She wanted her party to be simply the best,
So she had to be careful when choosing each guest.

I can't invite Pig. She'll eat all the food.
And Goat is always in such a bad mood!
I can't ask Dog. All he does is growl.
I know what I'll do. I'll ask the Wise Owl!

Who?
Owl, if Cat comes all she'll do is purr.
And she has that bad habit of licking her fur.

I see, Owl said, But what about Lamb?
What cried Goose. She's more boring than I am.

Sheep is too dumb, so I'd like to ask Horse,
But all he does is graze on green grass, of course.
No one is worse than that messy Raccoon
Except maybe Fox who just howls at the moon.
Arrooo!

There must be someone you'd like to come
But sadly Goose could think of no one.

The Turtle's too slow, he'd be late to arrive.
Duh, I'm here.
And that Bee is too busy to leave his beehive.
That silly Old Hen just keeps pecking a round,
And that Gopher keeps digging those holes in the ground!

What about Donkey?
No, he's such a dud.
Hee-haw!
All that Cow does is moo
And chew on her cud!
Moo!

I just can't stand that Rooster with that ratty hairdo,
Who just struts around going cock-a-doodle, cock-a-doodle,
cock-a-doodle-doodle-do!

By now Lucy Goosy was becoming alarmed.
Why I used to think I had good friends on this farm.
Well perhaps it's your fault said the Owl always wise.
All you seem to do well is criticize.

But if I invite Mouse, she'll mess up the house.
If I invite Rabbit, I'm sure he'll just blab it.
If I invite Ant, I'll get ants in my pants!
And if I invite Flea she might bite me!
Ouch!

The wise old owl simply shook his head.
Then he cleared his throat, and he gently said,
No one is perfect, you know, even you.
If you want my advice, this is what you should do . . .
Invite every animal on the farm to come!
When we all get together, it will be so much fun.
Oh, can't you imagine the look in their eyes,
When suddenly each comes to realize
Each one's been invited to share your special day?
No one will forget Lucy Goosy's birthday!

Lucy Goosy bowed her head in shame.
You mean each one is special because no one's the same?

Yes, each has a gift that no one else gives
So let's celebrate how different each one of us is!